D0690183

Newport Public Library
This discarded book needs
a new home.
We hope you enjoy it.

COVERED WAGONS, BUMPY TRAILS

For my wonderful mother-in-law, Florence,
whose self-sacrificing love envelops her family
with happiness and joy—V. K.

The art was done with watercolors and gouache on marbleized paper.

Text copyright © 2000 by Verla Kay. Illustrations copyright © 2000 by S. D. Schindler
All rights reserved. This book, or parts thereof, may not be reproduced in any form without permission in writing from the publisher. G. P. Putnam's Sons, a division of Penguin Putnam Books for Young Readers, 345 Hudson Street, New York, NY 10014. G. P. Putnam's Sons, Reg. U.S. Pat. & Tm. Off. Published simultaneously in Canada. Printed in Hong Kong by South China Printing Co. (1988) Ltd.
Designed by Gunta Alexander. Text set in Breughel.

Library of Congress Cataloging-in-Publication Data
Kay, Verla. Covered wagons, bumpy trails / written by Verla Kay ; illustrated by S. D. Schindler. p. cm. Summary: Illustrations and simple rhyming text follow a family as they make the difficult journey by wagon to a new home across the Rocky Mountains. [1. Overland journey to the Pacific—Fiction. 2. Frontier and pioneer life—Fiction. 3. Stories in rhyme.] I. Schindler, S. D., ill. II. Title.
PZ8.3.K225 Co 2000 [E]-dc21 96-37478 CIP AC ISBN 0-399-22928-0
1 3 5 7 9 10 8 6 4 2
First Impression

NEWPORT PUBLIC LIBRARY
NEWPORT, OREGON 97365

COVERED WAGONS, BUMPY TRAILS

Verla Kay illustrated by S. D. Schindler

G. P. PUTNAM'S SONS • NEW YORK

The California Trail
Independence, Missouri
LATE APRIL
MAY
Missouri River
Platte River
JUNE
Fort Laramie
Scott's Bluff
Chimney Rock
Independence Rock
Sweetwater R.
Ice Slough
JULY
ROCKY MOUNTAINS
Fort Bridger
Soda Springs
Sublette's Cutoff
Fort Hall
Oregon Trail
AUGUST
Hastings Cutoff
GREAT SALT LAKE
GREAT BASIN
Humboldt River
SIERRA NEVADA MOUNTAINS
SACRAMENTO VALLEY
SEPTEMBER

AUTHOR'S NOTE

Pioneers heading for California stuffed their wagons with furniture, clothes, and food. Along the way, fresh milk was churned into butter in pails hanging from the bouncing wagons. Wagon trains needed to reach Independence Rock by the Fourth of July to be on schedule, and the average speed of a fully loaded wagon was fifteen miles per day.

There was a permanent bed of ice under the ground at Ice Slough, and the pioneers chopped out big chunks for their water barrels. Sublette's Cutoff had no water for fifty miles so most pioneers took the longer, easier route past Fort Bridger. When they reached Soda Springs they could make lemonade from naturally carbonated water.

After passing Fort Hall, pioneers trudged through the white salt sands of the Great Basin. Then they struggled over the rugged Sierra Nevada mountains with great urgency so they would get across before winter snowstorms trapped them.

What a joyous sight it must have been for the weary pioneers when they finally reached the crest of the last mountaintop and looked down on the beautiful Sacramento Valley.

Covered wagon,
Bumpy road.
Plodding oxen,
Heavy load.

Mother, Father,
Baby John,
Bouncing, jouncing,
Moving on.

Fodder, water,
Guns and tools.
Clothes and blankets,
Stubborn mules.

Falter, flounder,
WHOOPS! In ditch.
Wiggle, wriggle,
Try a switch.

THUNDER! LIGHTNING!
Floods of rain.
Mucky, muddy,
Wet terrain.

Mother, Father,
Baby John,
Pushing forward,
Struggle on.

Weary, bleary,
Sweaty, hot.
End of day,
A camping spot.

Dry chips burning,
Steaks of snakes.
Coffee brewing,
Johnnycakes.

Rocky Mountains,
Massive, steep.
Rugged trail,
Wagons creep.

Dumping, tossing,
Trinkets, trunk.
Cookstove, treasures—
Now they're junk.

Hot sun swelters,
Parched land, dry.
Thick dust swirls,
Choking sky.

Mother, Father,
Baby John,
Plodding forward,
Struggle on.

Pushing, shoving,
Top of crest.
Fire, blankets,
Well-earned rest.

Frosty, frigid,
Icy air.
Lacy snowflakes
Everywhere.

Plunging, slipping,
Stuck in snow.
Frozen wheels,
"Oxen, WHOA!"

Mother, Father,
Baby John,
Walking slowly,
Trudging on.

NEWPORT PUBLIC LIBRARY
NEWPORT, OREGON 97365

Moving forward,
End of trail.
Meadows, poppies,
Soft brown quail.

Building cabins,
Clearing lands.
Rustic timbers,
Helping hands.

Mother, Father,
Baby John,
Fleecy flannel
Nightclothes on.

Sturdy windows,
Heavy doors.
Warm and safe now,
Happy snores.